I

s

GW00792423

Dr Tu
and the
Autumn Snooze

By the same author

Callender Hill Stories

Dr Twilite
and the
Autumn Snooze

ALEX SHEARER
Illustrated by Tony Kenyon

VICTOR GOLLANCZ
LONDON

To Kate and Nicholas

First published in Great Britain 1996
by Victor Gollancz
An imprint of the Cassell Group
Wellington House, 125 Strand, London WC2R 0BB

Text copyright © Alex Shearer 1996
Illustrations copyright © Tony Kenyon 1996

The right of Alex Shearer and Tony Kenyon
to be identified as authors of this work has
been asserted by them in accordance with the
Copyright, Designs and Patents Act, 1988

A catalogue record for this book is
available from the British Library

ISBN 0 575 06281 9

Photoset in Great Britain by
Rowland Phototypesetting Limited,
Bury St Edmunds, Suffolk
Printed by
Cox & Wyman Limited,
Reading Berkshire

96 97 98 99   10 9 8 7 6 5 4 3 2 1

Prologue

It was autumn in Callender Hill, and Sam and Lorna Walker's father was standing by the bedroom wardrobe, looking at what was left of his overcoat.

"It's the moths," he said. "Look what they've done to it. They've eaten all the good bits and there's only the sleeves left. And I can't just wear a pair of sleeves, can I? I'll look most peculiar."

"You should have put mothballs in the pockets," their mum told him.

"I did," he said. "They ate those too. I mean, you need a decent coat, come the autumn. I hope they haven't been at my socks as well."

"Well, make sure you keep the moths away from your wallet, Dad," Sam told him. "We don't want them eating our pocket money."

"Huh," he said. "I can see I'll get no sympathy here."

Sam and Lorna went to the kitchen then, to rummage in the cupboard and see what they could find to take to school for the Grown in My Garden display the next day. Children who lived in flats, or who didn't have gardens were allowed to cheat a little.

"How about this tin of cat food?" Lorna said. "Would that be all right?"

"I don't think cat food is quite what your headteacher has in mind," her mother said. "I think he more expects fruit and vegetables and things like that to put on the steps of the assembly hall. Things that *people* can eat."

"I'll maybe take some chewing-gum in then," Sam said. "I think I've got a bit somewhere, stuck to the leg of the bed."

In the end, Sam took a tin of sardines into school and Lorna took a tin of apricots, and these objects sat among the melons and apples in the display of autumn thanksgiving. And Sam and Lorna felt very proud and rather generous. Though in truth Sam hated sardines and Lorna didn't like apricots, so they were quite glad to get rid of them.

Sam wasn't sure if he liked autumn or not. It was a bit of a dismal season, what with the rain falling and the days getting shorter and the leaves dropping off the trees.

He liked Hallowe'en though, and he liked making pumpkin lanterns with scary faces and mouths of jagged teeth.

He and Lorna would get dressed up as ghosts and wizards, and put green and white paint on their faces, and maybe wear pointed hats with stars on, and stick on false noses and plastic warts. Then they would go out to do tricking or treating upon the neighbours in their block of flats.

"Trick or treat?" they said to old Mr Hendley in the flat down below. But his hearing wasn't so good, and he thought they had said, "How's your smelly feet?" and he told them not to be so rude and went to close the door on them.

"And why are you wearing those sheets?" he asked. "Don't your parents give you proper clothes? Or are you pretending to be beds?"

"No," Sam explained, "we're pretending to be ghosties. And you have to give us a treat or we play a trick on you."

"What sort of tricks do you do? Do you do card tricks?"

"No, no, naughty tricks—I think," Sam said, uncertainly. "Usually we never do any, as people always give us treats. I don't think we'd do any nasty tricks really. It's just pretend."

"Well, I'll give you a biscuit each," Mr Hendley said, "but it's not 'cause you frighten me. I'm not scared of ghosts. It's all in the past that kind of thing. Nothing exciting ever happens these days, except on the telly. No, nothing ever happens in the autumn," he told them. "It's the dullest season of them all."

But just because you say something, that doesn't mean you're right.

1

Perkins

"That squirrel," Dr Twilite said, "is nodding off again. Give him a poke in the ribs, would you, my love, to keep him lively, then send him off for a few more acorns. And chase after that tortoise too, when you have a moment. It looks to me like he's making a run for it."

"Right you are, my dear," Mr Twilite answered. "Just finish this notice." And he dipped his paintbrush into a pot of black ink and wrote on the piece of white card in front of him:

*Nearly New and Slightly Used
Birds' Nests For Sale.
Ideal Homes For Cuckoos or
Would Do For Soup.*

"I'll pin it up on the fence later," Mr Twilite said. "Now then—wakey, wakey!"

He leaned over and gave Perkins, their squirrel, a poke in the ribs with the paintbrush. It was a very gentle poke. More of a tickle than anything. Perkins opened his half-closed eyes, and looked about blearily as if to say:

"Who's doing that? And whoever it is, stop it!"

"Perkins," Mr Twilite said, "we're low on nuts. Nip out and get a few acorns in, there's a good chap. And see if there aren't any chestnuts around. People will pay top prices for good roasting chestnuts, and we have to make hay while the sun shines."

"But the sun isn't shining," Perkins's expression seemed to say. "It's autumn, and cloudy, and it'll soon be winter and time to—"

Nearly new and slightly used bird's nests for sale. Ideal home

And he yawned, opening his mouth so widely, that he could have got his whole tail in, and swallowed it. Which would have been quite a feat, as Perkins's tail was bigger than he was.

Mr Twilite gave him another prod.

"Come on, Perkins. This is no time to be going into hibernation," he said. "The season's work is barely started. You can't go to sleep yet."

Perkins stretched, scratched himself, took a sip of water from a cup on the desk, and hopped over to the window. Dr Twilite opened it for him.

"And best quality nuts, Perkins, remember," she reminded him. "And don't go eating too many. And don't go stashing nuts away in tree holes again, and then forget where you've put them. Oh, and Perkins—"

But he had hopped off over the fence, and was heading for the woods.

Dr Twilite watched him go.

"Right, well, I'd best get out myself," she said, "and gather up the morning's windfalls. I want to get to those apples before the worms do. And tomorrow we can make a start on the fallen leaves."

"Then there's the mushrooms and toadstools," Mr Twilite reminded her. "They'll be popping up soon."

"Yes," Dr Twilite agreed. "Autumn, it's the busiest time of the year."

"And the berries," Mr Twilite continued, "they'll want picking—"

"I know!" said Dr Twilite. "No need to remind me!"

"Well, no need to snap, I'm sure," Mr Twilite said.

Tempers always got a little short come the autumn, frayed like the cuffs on Dr Twilite's old coat. Everything about her was a bit ragged. Spotlessly clean, neatly darned and patched, but she was always just a little bit threadbare and second-hand, all held together with pins and sticking plaster.

"I hate anything new," she used to say. "Can't abide it. You remember that new skirt I bought once, my love? I didn't feel comfortable in it for years. But as soon as the seat was shiny and the buttons had popped off, why, I felt like a different person. And the day I had to sew a big patch on the seat of my old bloomers, I felt so happy I could have whistled. Whistled an

old tune that is—not a new one. I don't like these new tunes at all. They don't write them like they used to and they never did."

Dr and Mr Twilite had three children—all grown up now and left home—and their names were Morning Twilite, who had been born in the morning, Evening Twilite, who had been born in the evening, and Skylite Twilite, who had been born in the attic. But Dr Twilite hadn't liked them much when they were new either, though as they grew older she loved them dearly.

"It's not the noise," she said. "It's not the

nappies. It's not even the wind and the burps. It's because they're so *new* and shiny with those little bald heads. I just can't take to them, my dear. I'm sorry, but it's not my fault."

And try as she did, she found them very hard to get used to indeed.

"Do you really have to wash that baby quite so much, my dear," she would complain to Mr Twilite, "and dunk it in the bath so often? It takes all the character out of it, and makes it look unnatural. Couldn't you just give it a rub down with an oily rag? I'm sure it would be much better for it."

And it was really only when she could see her children out in the garden, covered in mud, or sitting at the kitchen table with their breakfasts all down their pyjamas and with bowls of

cereal on their heads, that Dr Twilite could take any pride or pleasure in them.

"They look like unmade beds, those kids!" Mr Twilite would mutter.

"Yes, aren't they wonderful? You can't beat an unmade bed," Dr Twilite would reply. "An unmade bed, and a sink full of unwashed dishes. Marvellous. That's what I like!"

Then she would go up and unmake all the beds which Mr Twilite had just made. For as well as hating new things, she hated too much order.

"Go and untidy your rooms," she would tell her children. "They don't look like pig-sties." And she would turn to her son, Skylite, who was irritatingly neat and say:

"Look at you, Skylite! You disgustingly tidy boy! Go and scruffy yourself up this instant! You're a disgrace! Is that a handkerchief you're using to wipe your nose on? What's wrong with your sleeve! Why don't you blow your nose on your pullover, like I told you? Have you got no manners at all?"

So Dr and Mr Twilite were often at logger-heads. For he liked things to be new and fresh, and she liked them to be old and seasoned. And he liked order and tidiness. And she liked disorder and for things to be natural. They were like Jack and Mrs Sprat in the old rhyme.

But for all that they were so different, they were also rather the same. Dr Twilite collected all the autumn things because she loved everything old and leathery. Mr Twilite collected all the autumn things because he wanted to tidy them up. And so they ended up, like many people, doing exactly the same things for totally different reasons.

And so it was that one day they gave up their jobs, took their life-savings out of the bank, moved house and rented a piece of land on the industrial estate. And thus the Autumn Reclamation, Leaf Recycling, Environmental Nut and Mushroom Storage Company was born.

2

Webs and Pats

At first Dr Twilite had just collected old newspapers, bottles and cans.

"But that's only to get started," she explained. "It's the stuff that other people *don't* recycle, that's what we need to work on. Maybe something can be made of it. I'm going out for a walk to think."

On her walk, Dr Twilite went through the park, where everything was covered in the dew of an autumn morning and half hidden in mist.

She returned home in a state of great excitement.

"I've got it!" she said.

"Got what, my dear?" Mr Twilite asked.

"Spiders' webs!" she told him.

"You've got spiders' webs? Where? Under your arm? Hang on, I'll get the broom and tidy you up."

"No, no, my dear. I mean spiders' webs—why don't we recycle them? There must be thousands of old empty ones out there, all going to waste."

"But what could we do with them?"

"Lots of things," Dr Twilite said. "We could wind them up on to bobbins and sell the silk. We could put them in frames and sell them as pictures. I'll get to work on it first thing in the morning."

So the next day, Dr Twilite went out and collected as many old spiders' webs as she could, and by the end of the week she had several bobbins of spider silk and a dozen webs framed for decoration.

She put a notice up outside the yard.

Best Quality Spider Silk For Sale.
Reconditioned Webs On Offer, Ideal For
Hair Nets and Tennis Rackets.

"That'll bring the customers in," she said to Mr Twilite.

"Well, you see to it that they wipe their shoes," he told her. "I don't want them messing

19

up our scrap yard, and treating the place like a tip."

But it didn't bring the customers in at all. Not one.

"What's gone wrong?" Dr Twilite asked. "It's such marvellous silk. Why won't people buy it?"

"If you ask me, it's because spiders are involved," Mr Twilite said. "Spiders give most people the willies. And people don't want the willies. No, you should drop the spiders bit, if you ask me."

"Well," Dr Twilite thought, "I don't want to deceive people. But . . ."

The next day another sign appeared.

Natural Recycled Silk for Sale.
Finest Quality.

And then people did take an interest. And when Dr Twilite got the spider silk woven into cloth and made up into scarves, silk stockings and silk shirts, they were soon selling all the webs they could collect.

"Where do you get such marvellous silk

from?" the customers would ask. "I thought you could only get silk like this from China."

"Ah ha," Dr Twilite winked, "that would be telling. But I can say this, it's all perfectly natural. It's one of nature's resources, and we've stopped it from going to waste."

After her success with the spiders' webs, Dr Twilite turned her attention to cow pats.

"I was out on one of my walks," she explained to Mr Twilite later, "when I came upon them."

"As long as you didn't step in them," he said. "Because they're very squashy, are cow pats. You step into a really deep one, the chances are you'll never get out again. Why, my Uncle Roger, now he got stuck in one once, and he couldn't get out for love nor money. He spent the whole weekend there—day and night—stuck in the cow pat, crying for help. 'Help, help!' he went. 'I'm stuck in a pooh!' And if it hadn't been for a farmer coming by, he might have died. Even as it was, the farmer couldn't pull him out on his own, and they had to rope Uncle Roger up to a tractor. And they yanked him clean out of his boots. But the boots themselves, they couldn't budge them. And, to this day, his boots are still stuck in that cow pat, as a warning to the unwary. And that," he rounded off, "is a true story. More or less. In places."

"Are you sure it's a true story, my love?" Dr Twilite asked doubtfully.

"Well, it's certainly a very tidy story," Mr

Twilite said. "But I'm sorry, did I interrupt you?"

"All I was going to say," she continued, "was it crossed my mind this morning that it's all such a dreadful waste. All the cow pats, that is. It seems to me that we should be trying to make some use of them. Trying to recycle them and to do our bit for the environment."

"Well, I'm not against a bit of tidying, as you know," Mr Twilite said. "But I can't really see what you could do with cow pats."

"I thought that maybe we could sell them as Frisbees," Dr Twilite suggested.

"Frisbees?" Mr Twilite murmured. "I don't know about that. I can't see people buying cow pats to use as Frisbees, to be honest, my love. They might fall apart when you threw them."

"How about hats then?" Dr Twilite said. "For weddings?"

"No, I can't see that either. Cow pat hats, no, I don't think people would buy them in any quantity at all."

"Then what about hot water bottles?" Dr Twilite said, trying the last of her ideas. "They'd surely keep your feet warm."

"Hot water bottles? No, my dear, I don't think people would much fancy warming the bed up with a cow pat. You could always try it—don't let me discourage you—but not in our bed if you wouldn't mind."

"It does seem such a shame," she said, "that they should go to waste."

A week later, Dr Twilite read in a magazine that when left to rot, cow pats gave off a gas called methane. And this gas could be used to run your heating. So she built a special adaptor, in order to use the cow pats for fuel, and this, at least, was a great success.

"And the marvellous thing is, it costs nothing," she said. "Other than the trouble of bagging up a few cow pats every day and bringing them home."

"It must make the fields look so much tidier too," Mr Twilite said approvingly. "Because I like a cow as much as the next person, but they aren't very fussy animals. Just chucking their pats everywhere and never clearing up after themselves. Shall I turn the heating down a bit, my love?" he added. "It's ever so hot in here."

"Warm as toast, my love."

"Warm as pats."

Then off Dr Twilite would go, to stock up on more fuel for the winter.

"And if you ever see a cow pat with a pair of boots stuck in it on your travels," Mr Twilite reminded her, "you'll know who they belong to."

"Your Uncle Roger?" she said.

"He's the one," Mr Twilite nodded, "he's the one."

So the Autumn Reclamation Company became more successful, and Dr Twilite grew happier, as she thought of more and more recycling schemes, and new ideas came to her almost daily.

She looked out of the window one morning at the garden and the woods beyond, at the leaves falling to the ground and at the berries growing wild on the bushes.

"What marvellous colours there are in

autumn," she thought. "All the greens and reds and browns and golds in a thousand variations. If only you could buy colours like that. Not artificial ones, but real true autumn colours."

Then she thought, "But why can't you?" And she rushed out into the garden, gathered up a few sackfuls of leaves, took them to her laboratory workshop, and put a beaker of water on the boil.

"Now let's see," she said, "if we can't get the colour out of them."

And she did. And before long another sign went up on the fence:

New Twilite Paint Range. Natural Autumn Colours. Mellow Yellow. Hint of Russet. See Inside For Full Selection.

The paints were an immediate success and were soon followed by a woodland range of make-up and toiletries called Dr Twilite's Autumnal Cosmetics. She sold Mushroom Moisturizer, Eau de Toadstool Perfume, Autumn Footpath Mud Packs and a wide selection of soaps. (Not tested on animals. Or vegetables either.) And these were quite a success too.

It was shortly after that when Perkins turned up. Mr Twilite had spotted him first.

"Look, my dear," he said. "There's a squirrel out by the chestnut tree. Just standing there, scratching his head."

"He looks to me like he's lost his nuts," Dr Twilite said.

"Looks to me," Mr Twilite said, "like he's lost his marbles."

"No, squirrels are always doing that," Dr Twilite explained. "Losing their nuts. They collect a big load, hide them away in a hole somewhere and then can't remember where they put them. But squirrels are dab hands at climbing trees. Dab legs too probably. I wonder if he's looking for a job."

As Perkins grew used to the Twilites, he began to come up to their window, and then into their kitchen. Then he started bringing them nuts.

"Tell you what, Perkins," Dr Twilite said. (Not that she had any reason to know his name was Perkins. It just seemed to suit him.) "If you want, I'll give you a job. You collect the nuts for me, and always bring them here. Then you won't have to worry about where you've left them, as I'll always have some put aside for you. And in return we'll give you a drink of milk every day, and a box to sleep in when you go into hibernation. How's that?"

She couldn't really be sure if Perkins understood, but he seemed to get the hang of it, and he brought nuts by the dozen to the house,

and they were all very pleased with the arrangement.

Once a few sacks of chestnuts had been collected by Perkins, Mr Twilite would get his dusters out and polish them till they shone. Then they would be sent up to London for the chestnut vendors to roast and to sell on the streets.

Now you might think that Dr Twilite would have been content by then, with all her enterprises, and happy to go on collecting chestnuts and cow pats and spiders' webs for the rest of her days. But no. For Dr Twilite was a restless spirit, and she believed that no matter how good things were, they could always be improved, and that there would always be new ways in which to make the world a better place. And that was when she had the fantabulous idea. And it was all thanks to Perkins the squirrel.

3

A Poke in the Acorns

"Give Perkins a little poke in the acorns, my dear," Mr Twilite said one late November evening. "I do believe he's snoozing off again."

Dr Twilite leant over and gave Perkins a gentle nudge in the ribs as he snored in the armchair. Perkins opened his eyes blearily, gave her a *where's my nuts?* sort of look, and dozed off again.

"No good," she said. "He's away. We'll get nothing out of him for weeks now. I might as well put him in his box and wait till spring."

Then she had the idea.

"What's the matter?" Mr Twilite asked. "Why are you staring like that?"

"It's Perkins!" Dr Twilite said. "Don't you see what he's doing!"

"He's not doing anything, is he? Apart from sleeping. He's gone into hibernation for the winter. Great furry ball of nothing, snoring away there like a set of hairy bagpipes."

"Exactly," Dr Twilite cried. "Gone into hibernation and he won't wake till spring. Just think, my dear, what if *we* could do that?"

"Do what?"

"Hibernate! Don't you see! We wouldn't be using electricity or eating dinners for months. We'd save so much of the world's resources. It would do wonders for the environment. Everything would last so much longer. We'd be able to share out everything all around the world. Poor people would have more, and rich people wouldn't need so much, as they'd be asleep for two months of the year. It's a splendid idea, don't you think?"

But Mr Twilite was uncertain. "I'm not so sure," he said. "I don't know . . ."

"Well, I do!" Dr Twilite said. "And I am going to try and do what Perkins is doing right now!"

"What? Sleep in a shoe box?" Mr Twilite said. "You're too big."

"No, no. I mean go into hibernation. Just to see if it can be done. I'll see you again in March, my dear. Or possibly at the end of February."

"But what about your Christmas presents?" Mr Twilite called after her as she headed up the stairs.

"I'll open them at Easter," Dr Twilite shouted back.

And the bedroom door closed behind her.

"You didn't hibernate for very long, did you?" Mr Twilite said, when Dr Twilite woke up at seven the next morning, the same as usual.

"I tried," she said. "But I must be doing something wrong. Maybe the room's not quiet enough. I'll try again tonight. Only this time I'll sleep in the loft."

So that evening Dr Twilite took her sleeping bag and went up to hibernate in the loft, along with Perkins, whose box she had put up there.

But she didn't hibernate very well. In fact, she hardly got a wink of hibernation all night. It was cold in the loft, and draughty, and the water tanks gurgled. She awoke at six the next morning, and was down in the kitchen long before Mr Twilite.

"Hello," he said. "What are you doing sitting

here drinking tea? I thought you were supposed to be hibernating."

"I was," Dr Twilite said. "Only I kept waking up. This hibernating business is trickier than it seems. You'd think anyone could do it, just lie in bed for weeks on end. But it's not that simple. How come I keep waking up but Perkins doesn't?"

"Ask him," Mr Twilite suggested.

"I can't," Dr Twilite said. "He's asleep. But there must be something inside squirrels that we haven't got in us. If only I could find out what it was, and turn it into a medicine. Then all we'd have to do is drink it, and we could hibernate too."

"You want to get a couple of old squirrels and a few old tortoises and boil them up then," Mr Twilite suggested. "Make a drop of soup out of them. Or a bit of ointment, and rub it on your chest. That'll do the trick."

But Dr Twilite shied away from such an idea.

"I couldn't do that," she said. "It's cruel. Anyway, why should it work?"

"Why shouldn't it?" Mr Twilite argued.

"You are what you eat. Look at flamingos. If they eat shrimps, it turns them pink. And my Uncle Roger, now he used to eat crabs. And after a while he ate so many of them he started to walk sideways. And then he moved out of his house and started to live in a big shell. And that's a true—"

But Dr Twilite was already on her way to her workshop.

"You are what you eat! Of course. That must be it! That's how squirrels and tortoises manage to sleep so long. It must be their diet!"

Over the next few days, Dr Twilite was busy trying to find the right recipe to send herself into hibernation.

"Squirrels like nuts, tortoises like lettuce, bears like honey and hedgehogs have fleas," she said. "So I'll try a lettuce, nut, flea and honey sandwich. That makes sense."

But instead of putting her to sleep, the sandwich kept her awake with a bad stomach all night, as she couldn't digest the raw acorns, and the fleas hopped out of the sandwich and ran off.

So she tried making acorn, lettuce and honey soup instead. And though it tasted better than the sandwiches, it still didn't work.

"Something's missing here. But what? Or maybe I've just got the quantities wrong. I'll try a different mixture," she thought.

And she started again.

She found an old tortoises's shell and used that for stock, then she dropped a few windfall apples in, half a cow pat, and a few mushrooms for luck. Then she left the mixture to sit overnight in a big jar in the workshop.

Only she forgot to tell Mr Twilite about it. So when he went in that evening to go round with his vacuum cleaner, he came across the jar of foul-smelling and evil-looking liquid as it bubbled away.

"Now look at that," he said. "That's not very tidy." He put his nose to the jar and took a sniff. "And it doesn't smell too good either. If there's one thing I can't stand it's—"

And he fell asleep.

Not for long. Only fifteen minutes or so. And when he woke, there he was, in the same place, still leaning on the vacuum cleaner.

"Strange," he said. "I've got the funniest feeling—almost as if I—" Then he saw the clock up on the wall.

"Oh my, I'm running late tonight," he thought. "Odd. It's almost as if I'd—nodded off. But I couldn't have. Yet the last thing I remember was taking a sniff of . . ."

He peered at the mixture in the jar.

"Nasty-looking stuff," he mused. "Definitely needs tidying up. I'd better dispose of it thoughtfully, like they say on drinks cans."

So he picked up the jar of hibernation mixture and carried it outside.

"I won't put it down the drain," he thought, "as it might be bad for the pipes. So what would be a tidy way of getting rid of it?"

He looked around the garden, and his eyes lit on the old well, down by the compost heap. It was covered over with planks and heavy stones, and it was very deep and dark.

"Now that might be the answer. Tip it down there. That won't do any harm to anyone."

Dr Twilite didn't notice that her mixture had gone until the next morning, and by then

36

it was too late to get it back.

She was very annoyed. "Where's my mixture?" she demanded. "My hibernation special!"

"Is that what it was?" Mr Twilite said. "Well, I've tidied that away."

Dr Twilite knew full well what that meant.

"I didn't want it tidied away!" she grumbled. "You're always tidying my things away! One day you'll tidy me away, and I'll never see myself again. And where's my breakfast?"

"Too late," Mr Twilite told her, "it's been tidied away."

Dr Twilite groaned. "I'll have to start on my mixture all over again now," she said. "Where exactly did you tidy it away to?"

"I poured it down the old well," Mr Twilite said. "Best place for it. You shouldn't go making up funny mixtures. They can be dangerous."

Dr Twilite went out into the garden to stop her temper getting the better of her. After a few minutes she calmed down, and went to look at the old well. The cover had been replaced and the stones put back on top of it.

But Dr Twilite noticed a strange thing. In a circle around the well, everything had gone to sleep. Spiders were snoring in their webs; worms were asleep in the earth, with just the tips of their tails poking out; ants were dozing; snails had ground to a halt.

"My hibernation mixture!" she cried. "It worked! I must have got it right! It's put everything nearby to sleep! And now it's gone and I didn't write down the recipe. Oh, drat, drat, drat! I'll have to start all over again."

And she went to her workshop in a very bad mood and slammed the door behind her. Twice. Loudly. So that Mr Twilite would be sure to hear.

Now, that might have been the end of the matter, only the old well was not just a stagnant pool, as Dr and Mr Twilite believed. On the contrary, it led to an underground spring, and the spring led to the river, and the river led to the reservoir. And the reservoir led to the water taps of every house in the town of Callender Hill.

So as the water flowed along on its journey, it carried Dr Twilite's hibernation mixture with it. Of course, by the time it got to the reservoir, it was diluted enormously, but the hibernation mixture was so strong that even a tiny drop in a great big lake was enough to put a whole town to sleep.

A drop in your coffee, a drop in your tea, a drop in your orange squash, just the merest taste in your lemon barley water and—

Zzzzzzzzzz . . . Till spring.

Now Dr and Mr Twilite did not drink the water from the taps. Not because they had anything against it, but because Dr Twilite had a water supply of her own.

"Waste not, want not, and save it if you can, that's my motto," she said.

So Dr Twilite had set up her own water-collecting scheme using a series of pipes and gutters to gather rainwater as it fell. It was then pumped up from a barrel to a tank at the top of the house.

"Taste the freshness!" she'd say. "That stuff from the water board's all right, but you can't beat it straight from the sky. One day every house will have everything it needs. Everyone will be self-sufficient. Just like us."

But that day was yet to come. And down in Callender Hill, the people still relied on the reservoir to provide their tap water. And everyone drank water, more or less. Though sometimes they liked a change.

4

The Tree Mugger

"Coke!" Sam said.

"Pepsi for me!" Lorna said, just to be different.

"No, I've changed my mind, Dad," Sam said. "On second thoughts, I won't have a drink, I'll have a soft ice-cream."

"Me too," said Lorna, to be the same. "And can I have a flake?"

"Then again, Dad," Sam said, "maybe I'll have a hot dog and chips."

The man in the ice-cream van was looking fed up.

"Are they having anything or not? I have got other parks to go to."

"Give them two orange ice lollies," Dad said. He turned to Sam and Lorna. "There, I've decided for you."

The man gave Dad two orange lollies, which

he paid for and handed to Lorna and Sam. They peeled off the wrappers and put them— he was pleased to see—in the bin, without even being asked.

"Your change," the man said, giving Dad his money. "And it's as good as a rest."

"What is?"

"Change. It's as good as a rest. It's a joke. Ha ha."

Then the ice-cream van sped away in a cloud of filthy black exhaust fumes, leaving them all coughing and spluttering. A sign at the back of the van read: "Mind That Child."

Once they had their lollies, Sam and Lorna returned to their mission. This was the reason they had come to the park, to collect chestnuts to take home and roast in the oven.

"Can you get any more chestnuts down, Dad?" Sam said. They had only collected two so far.

"I'll try," Dad said. He took a heavy stick and threw it up into the tree. It fell through the branches, but it didn't bring a single chestnut down with it.

"I think someone must have got here before

us," he said. "And they've had the lot."

And he was right there. Not that he knew it was the Autumn Storage Company and its favourite employee, Perkins the squirrel, who were responsible.

"Or maybe it's just a bad year for chestnuts," he added. "Here, I'll try once more and if that doesn't work we'll just have to go and buy some."

He picked up the stick and was about to throw it into the branches when a shrill but strong voice carried across the park.

"Stop that at once, you vandal!" it shouted. "How dare you attack that poor tree! Leave it alone or I'll have the police on you!"

Lorna and Sam looked up to see a small, elderly lady bustling across the park towards them. An even smaller, and equally elderly, dog bustled along behind her.

"Stop it this instant!" the old lady shouted. "Yes, you!" she said to Dad. "It's you I'm talking to, you bully! Leave that poor tree alone."

So surprised was he, Dad dropped the stick. As he did, the old lady's dog grabbed it in its mouth and ran off with it across the park.

"Well done, Tiddles," she called. "You've disarmed him!" Then she turned to Dad and raised her fists.

"Come on then, you coward," she said. "Let's see how brave you are when you haven't got your stick. Want a fight, do you? Well, put them up."

Sam looked at Lorna. "Great!" he said. "Dad's getting into a punch-up!"

Dad was looking confused. The old lady stood in front of him with her fists up and her handbag on her arm, seeming as if she might bonk him on the nose at any second.

"Defend yourself, you coward," she said. "Come on, you thug!"

"Em—" Dad began.

"Go on, Dad!" Sam yelled. "Wallop her! She's only little!"

The old lady kept her fists up.

"I may be little," she said, "but I'm tough. And I happen to have a black belt in judo. And a black handbag in thumping. I also have some black tights. But I only wear them to funerals."

The old lady's dog had returned now—

minus the stick—and was standing by, snarling and trying to look ferocious. But it wasn't really much of a natural at it, and gave up after a couple of snarls.

"Well done, Tiddles," the old lady said. "You've hidden his stick. Good boy."

Dad shuffled uneasily.

"No sudden moves," the old lady warned him. "Or you're a dead man."

"Would you mind my asking," he said, "what this is all about?"

"What's it about!" the old lady—who was called Miss Endicott—cried. "Don't play the innocent with me! You know perfectly well what it's about. I saw you attacking that poor defenceless tree with that big stick! Mugging it, you were. Yes, you're a tree mugger. You were mugging it for its nuts."

"I wasn't," Dad said. "I was only trying to get a few chestnuts down—"

"Ah! So you admit it! Mugging a tree for its chestnuts—why, you'll be snatching old ladies' handbags next." She glanced at her own handbag. "Don't get any ideas," she added.

"But all I was doing—" Dad tried to say. But that was as far as he got.

"Are these your children?" Miss Endicott demanded, pointing at Lorna and Sam. "The ones with the orange tongues?"

"Yes, they are, as a matter of fact—" Dad began.

"Then you ought to be ashamed of yourself, for setting such a bad example. How are these children ever going to grow up with proper standards when they see their own father attacking trees with sticks!"

"I wasn't attacking it!" Dad wailed. "I was just trying to get a few chestnuts down!"

"Ha! That may be what you call it, but you don't fool me," Miss Endicott said. "I know a right thug when I see one. Just look at you. Even your eyebrows look stolen! And wherever did you get that nose from!"

Dad had a feeling that there was not much point in arguing with Miss Endicott. He had met her before in the park, and had always come out the loser from their encounters. All the same, he felt upset at being so misjudged.

"We weren't doing any harm," he said. "I was just trying to get a few chestnuts down for my children."

"Then you should feed them properly, you selfish brute," Miss Endicott said. "Not expect them to live on chestnuts."

"But they don't—"

"Why, the poor famished waifs. Look at their thin, pinched faces and their orange tongues. Now that's a sign of ill health, if ever I've seen one."

"They haven't got pinched faces!" Dad said. "Who'd pinch faces like that! And as for their tongues—"

Miss Endicott wasn't listening. She was

rummaging in her handbag. She took out two pound coins, and handed one each to Sam and Lorna.

"There you are," she said, "you poor starved mites. There's a pound apiece. Go and get yourselves a nice hot bag of chips, and don't give any to your father. I wouldn't be surprised if it's him who's had all the cow pats too."

"Cow pats?" said Sam, looking up from the pound coin in his hand. "But you can't roast cow pats, not like chestnuts. You could put them in the toaster maybe—"

"No, no," Miss Endicott said. "I mean for the garden. Cow pats are wonderful things for the vegetables. Get your vegetables down in the autumn, cover them over with a few cow pats or a drop of horse manure. Pat your cow pats down and it'll keep them warm all winter. Then come the spring you'll have potatoes the size of melons."

"How would you get them in your mouth if they were the size of melons?" Sam asked.

"You'd cut them up, of course, you stupid boy," Miss Endicott snapped, eyeing Sam suspiciously, and wondering if she should take her pound back. "As you would know, if your father had taught you any table manners. Though by the look of him he probably hasn't."

"I think we should be going," Dad said, edging towards the gate.

"Well, I tell you," Miss Endicott said, "it's not good enough. Two hours I've been going round the fields, and how many cow pats did I find? Not one. So I came into the park on the off-chance that a stray cow might have wandered in and left one behind. Have you seen any cows?"

"Cows?" said Sam. "In the park? Why would you get cows in a park?"

"I don't know," Miss Endicott said. "Maybe they just got a bit frisky and fancied a go on the swings."

"No," said Lorna. "We'd have noticed. I mean, you'd remember a thing like that, a cow on the swings."

Sam and Lorna edged nearer to the park gates as well.

"Well, thanks for the pound," Lorna said.

"Very kind of you."

"We must be going, though," Sam said. "So, bye, then."

"OK," Dad shouted. "Now run for it!"

Then Sam and Lorna and their father turned on their heels and ran from the park as fast as they could, and they didn't look back once.

Miss Endicott stood watching them go. Tiddles, her dog, also gazed after the three disappearing figures. She looked down at him.

"What odd people, Tiddles," she said. "I wonder why they ran away like that. Maybe they needed the toilet. There's a lot of strange people around. You're not safe anywhere these days. Especially when you're old and frail, like me, and starting to lose your—what is it again I'm losing?"

"Woof!" said Tiddles.

"Oh yes, that's it, your memory. Yes, I think we'll have to go carefully, Tiddles, or we could end up having our handbags snatched."

"Woof, woof!" said Tiddles, as if to draw attention to the fact that he didn't actually have a handbag.

"And what's more," Miss Endicott said,

"just to be on the safe side, I think it might be best to make a run for it! *Go!*"

So saying, Miss Endicott leapt into action and ran off out of the park, her grey hair flying and her hat nearly coming off. Tiddles ran behind her, his four legs moving with great speed. Indeed they seemed to move faster than he did and, once or twice, they almost overtook him, and he had to bark at them to come back.

On they ran, as if a whole band of robbers were after them, and they didn't stop until they got to the police station, where they sprinted up the steps, ran into the enquiries office, ran up to the counter, and ran impatiently on the spot, while Miss Endicott banged on the bell.

After a moment, a large, mournful-looking policeman with sad eyes emerged from a back room and approached the desk, taking out his notebook as he did so.

When he saw who was waiting for him, his eyes looked even sadder.

"Might I enquire," he said, "why your legs are going up and down like that? And why are that dog's paws going round like paddles?"

"Never mind my paws," Miss Endicott said. "Who's pinched all the cow pats? That's what I want to know."

"You know," Sergeant Porter said, "I think I'm getting a headache. Could you come back next week?"

5

Sleeping Beauties

Now the Great Hibernation Mixture didn't get into the town's drinking water supply immediately. It took quite some time for it to seep from the well into the underground spring, and then to be carried along by the river to the reservoir. Then it had to make its way along the water pipes and finally into people's drinks.

Even then, the mixture had to build up inside people. For a small amount just made you feel dozy, but didn't really put you to sleep at once. But the bigger the dose, the dozier you got, until you got so dozy, you dozed off good and proper. And once you dozed off, you were done for.

So little by little and drop by drop the Great Hibernation Mixture found its way along the water pipes and into every house and every person.

It was so diluted that there was hardly any difference in the colour of the water. Although some people, with very sensitive taste buds, could detect a slight change in flavour.

"Hmm," they'd say. "I don't know, but it seems to have a different tang to it today, this water. It tastes a bit—sleepy."

"Sleepy?" their friends would say. "How can anything taste sleepy? You mean it tastes of old pyjamas? Or bedroom slippers?"

"No, I just mean that it seems a bit—yawny."

"Yawny? It tastes yawny?"

"Yes. It tastes a bit of—yawns."

"Big yawns, or little yawns?"

"Oh, you know, just—yawns."

And nobody believed them at all.

But believe it or not, the people in the town began to yawn more, and then to find themselves dozing off at odd moments in the afternoon.

"Just having a bit of a cat-nap," they said.

"Just having a bit of a person-nap," their cats miaowed to each other, as they too closed their eyes.

And so that was how the Great Hibernation Mixture began to work—trickle by trickle, yawn by yawn and sigh by sigh, until everybody fell asleep, all at once, at 11.23 one Tuesday morning.

Sergeant Porter reached for his glass of water and took a long swig.

Miss Endicott had returned.

"Yes, now it's about these cow pats," she was saying. "I was in last Saturday to complain about them, and I'm back to see what progress has been made. There's a cow pat thief about, I'm certain of it, and it's time that measures were taken. You want to get a bloodhound on the case to sniff the culprits out."

Sergeant Porter yawned. He looked up at the time. Even the hands of the clock seemed to be moving slowly, with great squeaky ticks and long grating tocks. Maybe they needed oiling.

Miss Endicott saw that Sergeant Porter was yawning.

"Do you know, I can see right down to your boots!" she told him.

Then, unable to stop herself, she yawned

too. And at her feet, Tiddles yawned as well.

"Tiddles," she said. "Put your paw in front of your mouth, there's a polite dog."

Ever obedient, Tiddles went to raise a paw up to his mouth. But at that moment a great

dog-like weariness came over him, as if he was tired of it all—all the barking and woofing and chasing sticks and begging for biscuits and playing dead. He felt as if he didn't want to be a dog any more, and all he really wanted to be was a statue of a dog. His eyes began to close, and his breathing grew deeper, and the next thing he knew, he didn't know anything. And a statue was what he had become.

"Good heavens," Miss Endicott said. "Look at that! He's nodded off."

"Maybe he thinks it's his bedtime," Sergeant Porter suggested.

"He doesn't have bedtime," Miss Endicott said. "He has baskettime. Tiddles!" she called. "Wake up! It isn't time to go to sleep yet. You haven't had your bowl of cocoa and your worming tablets."

But by way of reply, Tiddles started to snore.

"That dog," Sergeant Porter said, "is snoring. Snoring dogs are not allowed in the police station, as they compromise the dignity of the premises. Also, in my experience, wherever there are dogs with snores, there are dogs with wind not far behind. So I must ask you to re—"

Then the great tiredness came over Sergeant Porter too, as though he hadn't slept for years. His eyelids felt as heavy as handcuffs, and though he told himself that he must try to stay awake, in fact his last words were:

"I just need a strong cup of coffee to perk me up—"

There was nothing he could do to stop himself, and his eyes closed like curtains, and everything went black.

For a second it seemed as if he might fall over. He swayed from side to side, like a skittle you didn't quite knock over. But then he settled down and just stood by the desk, fast asleep.

"Now look," Miss Endicott was saying, "what about these stolen cow pats? Maybe you should arrest one of the cows and take her in for milking. Questioning, I mean. Or—"

Sergeant Porter began to snore. It was a massive snore, about the size of eight or nine footballs, all stuck together. It quite drowned out Tiddles's small, rasping snore, and made it seem like no more than a whistle.

Miss Endicott leaned across the desk.

"Hello!" she said. "Shop!" She banged on Sergeant Porter's head with the handle of her umbrella. "I say," she said, "anyone in there? Or have you moved out?"

But there was not a flicker, and Sergeant Porter went on snoring.

Miss Endicott prised one of his eyelids open.

"Am I boring you?" she said. "Because if I am, there are politer ways of telling a person than simply nodding off—" But she had to break off as a big yawn took hold of her. It was one of those really mighty yawns that come over you sometimes, usually during a church sermon, or in assembly at school. And though you try not to yawn the yawn, there is really nothing you can do to stop it, because it is more like the yawn is yawning you.

"My, my!" Miss Endicott said when the yawn was over. "That certainly rattled my jewellery. I can't think why I feel so tired. It's almost as if some kind of sleeping sick—"

And that was the last she knew. Her eyes closed, and a small, lady-like snore of the utmost daintiness and clarity came from her, so tiny and sweet and tuneful, it was more like a bird song than a snore.

Rumble-rumble-gurgle-snort, went Sergeant Porter.

Woofetty-snurkle-woofetty, went Tiddles.

Tinky-tinkety-tink, went Miss Endicott.

Ring, ring, went the telephone on the desk as it suddenly sprang into life. It rang and rang. But no one was awake to answer it and, finally, it fell asleep itself.

In Lorna Walker's class at school, it was storytime.

"And they all lived happily ever after!" Miss Conway said, and with a firm snap, she closed the book.

Lorna's hand shot up.

"Miss! Please! Can I ask a question?"

Now, if Miss Conway had been allowed to give an honest reply to that, it would have been "No, Lorna, you can't!" Because the trouble with Lorna Walker's questions was that they were often extremely difficult to answer. So right at that moment, with break-time only five minutes away, she might have preferred Lorna's hand to be down in her lap rather than up in the air. But as Lorna was a pupil and as

Miss Conway was a teacher, and as teachers are supposed to answer pupils' questions, she said:

"Yes, Lorna? What is it?" And made a big effort not to yawn.

"It's about the story we've just had, Miss, *Sleeping Beauty*. I've heard it before and what I don't understand is why didn't they all fall over?"

"I'm sorry, Lorna?"

"In *Sleeping Beauty*, Miss. It says that when she pricked her finger she fell asleep, and everyone in the house fell asleep too, at what they were doing. But why didn't any of them fall over?"

Miss Conway sighed, and then yawned. Why did she feel so tired? She noticed that several children had been yawning too. Maybe the room was too stuffy. She opened a window. A sharp blast of chilly autumn air came in. She yawned again. Lorna Walker was still asking questions.

"And another thing, Miss," she said. "When Prince Charming comes along and kisses Sleeping Beauty—why does it wake her up?"

"Yes, Miss," Carol Thewes chipped in. "Why did it wake her up? Did his breath smell? Had he been eating pickled onions?"

"And did they really live happily ever after, Miss?" Hugh Marks wanted to know. "Or did they just start having arguments?"

"Miss, if Sleeping Beauty was asleep for years and years, what did she do about going to the toilet?" Lorna asked.

But thankfully the bell went for break-time.

"I'll answer all those questions later," Miss Conway told them. "Don't forget to remind me. Now go and have your milk."

And she went off to the staff room, hoping by the time she came back that the children would have forgotten all about Sleeping Beauty, and that they could get on with some arithmetic instead.

Break was over.

In the classroom next to Lorna's, her brother Sam sat at the desk he shared with Simone Drew. One of the Ritter twins and Josh Simson sat behind him.

"OK," Mr Stewart, their teacher, said.

"We've all had a break, so let's get on."

It was funny, he usually felt wide awake and raring to go after his morning coffee, but today he just felt so—tired. And it was strange that the children in his class were yawning too. Because after a drink of milk and a brisk run about the playground, they were usually quite lively and refreshed.

"OK," he said. "Brighten up, you lot. It's not bedtime yet. Now, who knows what season it is?"

"Autumn, Mr Stewart."

"And who knows what happens in the autumn?"

"The leaves fall off the trees, Mr Stewart. And it's Hallowe'en!"

"And you roast chestnuts, and have thanksgiving, and do trick or treat."

"And who knows what some animals do?"

"They fall asleep!" Sam Walker said, and he gave a yawn, as if showing how to do it. "For the winter. And they don't wake up till spring."

"And why do they do that?" Mr Stewart asked.

"Because they're bonkers," Anton Ritter said.

"Because they're dead lazy!" Tony Ritter suggested.

"Because there's not much to eat in the winter, that's why," Simone said.

"Exactly," Mr Stewart said. "Some animals go to sleep in the winter to conserve energy! And who knows which animals do this?"

"Bears!" Sam said. "And squirrels."

"Quite right, Sam."

"And hedgehogs!"

"Quite right, Mary. Anything else?"

"And teachers!"

"No, Anton, teachers stay awake all year round. Believe it or not."

"So why are you yawning, Mr Stewart?" Tony Ritter demanded.

"I'm not, I'm just stretching my jaws to keep them fit. Now, who knows what it's called when animals go to sleep until springtime?"

"It's called having a kip, Mr Stewart!"

"No, Anton, not quite. Any other suggestions?"

"Having a big snooze, sir?"

"No, Carol. Sam?"

"I know, Mr Stewart. I've got it. It's called—called—hi—hi—"

"Yes, Sam, go on, I think you're there."

"It's called—hi—hi—hiber—hibernat—"

But Sam never did manage to finish what he was going to say. Because his head slumped down on to his desk and a second later he was fast asleep. And so was everyone else. Even Mr Stewart, at the front of the class. He stood there, swaying gently, like a tree in a breeze, his eyes tightly shut.

But just as in *Sleeping Beauty*, he did not fall over. He remained as if rooted to the floor. And the clock ticked behind him and the hands moved on towards lunchtime. Only lunchtime never came. Or rather it came and went unnoticed. There was just a strange and eerie stillness everywhere, and the drone of distant snoring.

6

Gone a Bit Quiet

Dr Twilite looked up from her work.

"Gone a bit quiet," she said.

She was at the end of the yard, wondering how she could recycle a large heap of Hallowe'en pumpkins, which grinned up at her with scorched faces and broken teeth, and with the tops of their heads sliced off.

"Sorry, my love?" Mr Twilite said, looking up from his nut polishing.

"I said," Dr Twilite repeated, "that it had all gone a bit quiet. Listen."

Mr Twilite listened. And yes it had gone quiet. Very quiet indeed.

"No cars," Dr Twilite observed. "No lorries. No buses. Nothing."

"Hmm," Mr Twilite agreed. "How odd. It's not just an ordinary silence that. It's more what I'd call an eerie one."

"I think," Dr Twilite said, "that I might pop into town to investigate. Maybe someone's invented a noise recycling machine, and if they have, I want a look at it."

A gleam came into her eye then.

"Just think," she said, "what you could do with all the recycled noise. All the noisy trucks and the people next door shouting at each other, you could turn it into peace and quiet and tinkling streams. Why, if a machine like that hasn't been invented, I'll invent it myself. Come on, let's get the bicycle."

The Twilites didn't own a car. But they had several bicycles, all made from bits of other bicycles, which had grown old and fallen apart, and so the wheels on them were often of different sizes. One of the bikes was a tandem, a bicycle made for two—well, for three really, two people and a squirrel. For on the back of it, Dr Twilite had fixed a small seat for Perkins, along with a tiny pair of pedals, so that he could pull his weight. And they used this bicycle when they all wanted to go off somewhere together.

There was also a special shopping bicycle

which Dr Twilite had assembled from old bicycle parts and a supermarket trolley. On this she could cycle to the supermarket, cycle inside, cycle up and down the aisles, fill up the trolley, cycle to the check-out, pay for everything, and cycle home again, all without getting off once. She was a well-known figure in the shops around town, and was known as the Cycling Recycler.

So Mr Twilite got the tandem ready, while Dr Twilite went looking for Perkins. She found him just about to doze off in front of the recycled TV, watching repeats of a programme called *Mrs Nutkins*. She gave him a poke.

"You can't go nodding off yet, Perkins," she told him. "If you're going to spend your whole life snoozing, there wasn't a lot of point in being born, was there? Maybe you should get yourself a badge with 'Born To Snooze' written on it. Come on, Perkins. We're going into town."

Perkins and the Twilites got on to the tandem. Dr Twilite had made their bicycle clips from old elastic bands, which had been re-twanged with her special re-twanging machine. And when the three of them were ready, they rode into town.

Callender Hill was like a town of waxworks. People were standing everywhere, all looking very lifelike, but none of the figures moved.

A traffic warden was asleep by a meter, in the middle of writing out a parking ticket. A hundred metres away, a motorist had fallen asleep while running to move his car. A policeman had dozed off as he gave directions to a stranger, his arm pointing down the street.

The traffic everywhere had whooshed to a lazy stop, fortunately without a single accident. The drivers were asleep at the wheels. The car engines had stalled, or run out of fuel, and all were silent.

In the burger bar, the assistants in their striped uniforms had fallen asleep as they poured out the milkshakes and shovelled up the fries. Customers sat at the tables, half-eaten burgers in their hands. In the supermarket, the cashiers slept at the check-outs. Workmen snored by holes in the road. Dr and Mr Twilite and Perkins the squirrel rode on, searching for signs of life.

"Definitely a bit quiet today," Dr Twilite said.

"Not what you'd call a lot going on," Mr Twilite agreed. "It reminds me of my Uncle Roger, the time his leg went to sleep, and the doctor told him that the best thing to do when your leg goes to sleep is to shout at it to wake it up and so he—"

"You know," Dr Twilite said, "I hate to interrupt one of your very interesting and true stories, my dear, but there's something not right here."

"Yes, I was thinking that," Mr Twilite agreed. "It does seem odd that everyone's asleep—especially in the middle of the day. Most peculiar."

"Yes," Dr Twilite said. "Why, it's almost as if everybody had—"

"Had what?"

"Gone into hibernation."

Mr Twilite thought of the jar of hibernation mixture then, which he had poured down the well, and he felt himself blush all over, right down to his recycled oatmeal socks, which had been made from lumps of old porridge.

"Hibernation?" he gulped. "How could they have gone into—hibernation?"

A look of suspicion crossed Dr Twilite's face.

"Tell me, my dear," she said. "Do you think it might have something to do with my Great Hibernation Mixture?"

"Great Hibernation Mixture?" Mr Twilite said. "Em—what hibernation mixture was that?"

"The one which I lost the recipe for and could never make again, and which certain persons tidied away and POURED DOWN THE WELL!"

"Oh, *that* one, *that* hibernation mixture. Yes, I vaguely remember something about it now you mention—"

"Down the well!" Dr Twilite moaned. "Of all the places to put it! It must have got into the drinking water! And everybody's gone and swallowed some—and—oh dear, oh dear, oh recycled dear!"

"But wasn't that what you wanted, my love? Didn't you say it would be a good idea if we all hibernated?"

"Yes. But the mixture was only at the experimental stage. It might send people to sleep for half an hour. It might send them to sleep for ever. And you can't just send people off into hibernation, not without asking them if they want to go first."

She thought quickly.

"Stop the bicycle!" she cried. "We'd better try and wake them up. And give Perkins a poke in the acorns. We don't want him nodding off too, or there'll just be us left with our eyes open."

So they stopped the bicycle, poked Perkins in the acorns, and then chose someone to try to wake up.

"Her!" Dr Twilite said. "Over there."

It was a middle-aged lady, who had fallen asleep on her way home with two bags of shopping. Dr Twilite tapped her on the shoulder.

"Excuse me, madam!" she said. "I hope we're not disturbing you, but you seem to have nodded off in the street."

She gave the woman a good shake, but she remained fast asleep.

"Tickle her!" Mr Twilite suggested. So they got hold of Perkins and tickled the woman under the chin with his tail. She sneezed but didn't budge.

"Shout in her ear," Mr Twilite suggested. "Worth a try."

"Right," Dr Twilite said. "Together."

"Wakey wakey!" they bellowed, one in each ear. An orange fell out of the woman's shopping bag, but she didn't wake up.

"I know," Dr Twilite said. "You'd better give her a kiss."

"Me!" Mr Twilite looked shocked. "Give her a *what*?"

"A kiss. You know. Like in *Sleeping Beauty*. Prince Charming gives Sleeping Beauty a kiss and it wakes her up. So give her a kiss."

"But I don't even know her," Mr Twilite objected. "You can't go round kissing people you don't even know. Can you?"

"Prince Charming didn't know Sleeping Beauty, but it didn't stop him."

"But I couldn't go kissing other ladies, my dear, I'm married to you."

"True," Dr Twilite said. "And normally I wouldn't suggest it. But this is an emergency. So go on—give her a smacker on the chops. You have my permission."

"All right, my dear, if you insist. I'll just get myself puckered up. I hope I can remember how to do this. I'm a bit rusty on the old kissing."

Mr Twilite got himself puckered, and he leant over and gave the lady a kiss on the cheek. A real smacker it was too, with a good slurp to it, and a loud plop at the end.

"Anything?" he said. "Any signs of life?"

"No," Dr Twilite said. "Not a flicker."

"Funny, it worked for Prince Charming,"

Mr Twilite said. "Let me try again."

"No, that's quite enough," Dr Twilite said. "Let's go home to think things over and decide on our next step."

So Dr and Mr Twilite and Perkins the squirrel clambered back on to the tandem, and cycled home to the scrap yard.

"Perkins isn't doing his share of the pedalling," Mr Twilite complained. "He's dozing off again. Give him a prod in the chestnuts."

So they gave Perkins a prod in the chestnuts until he did his share of the pedalling, and in ten minutes they were home.

"OK," Dr Twilite said. "Thinking-cap time. This is the situation as I see it. The hibernation mixture's got into the drinking water. Everyone's drunk some and fallen asleep. We have our own water, so we're unaffected. And as long as we don't drink the tap water, we'll be all right.

"Now the problem is how are we to wake everyone up? And if we can't wake them up until spring, what do we do with them? We can't leave them out in the streets, they'll freeze. So before we do anything else, we have to get back into town, wrap them up in something warm, and then start taking them home and putting them to bed. Then, when they're all safe we'll have to find a way of waking them. So first things first, and the first thing is—Operation Wrap Up."

"But what do we wrap everyone up with?" Mr Twilite said. "There must be hundreds of people out there. We haven't got that many blankets."

"We don't need blankets," Dr Twilite explained. "We'll use old newspapers. We've got stacks of them. I knew they'd come in handy."

"Newspapers? Will they keep you warm?"

"Oh yes," Dr Twilite said. "A few newspapers up your jumper will keep the cold out nicely. Come on, let's get to work."

So they loaded up their bicycle's saddle-bags with newspapers and cycled off to wrap everyone up before the frost settled in.

Back and forth they went, back and forth.

"It's hard work stuffing newspapers up people's jerseys," Mr Twilite said. "And getting it up their trouser legs is even harder. To be honest—I feel I'm taking liberties."

He was putting an old copy of the *Beano* up the Lord Mayor's trousers at the time.

"Staying warm," Dr Twilite said, "is more important than looking dignified. Now, if everyone's wrapped up, we can see about getting them off the streets. We'd better start with the smaller ones. Babies and children and mothers with toddlers first."

Dr and Mr Twilite looked for people's names and addresses in their wallets or purses, and then set about taking them home and putting them to bed.

"You take their ankles," Dr Twilite instructed her husband, "I'll take their shoulders,

Perkins can help with their big toes, and off we go."

Sometimes they got people mixed up and took them to the wrong houses. Sometimes they couldn't find a name or address, and just had to make a guess.

They found Miss Endicott in the police station, alongside Sergeant Porter, and they thought that maybe she was Sergeant Porter's mum, so they took them both back to Miss Endicott's house—along with Tiddles the dog—and sat Miss Endicott in an armchair, and put Sergeant Porter on the sofa (he was too big to fit on a chair) and set Tiddles on a rug by the fireplace.

"Should be all right in here," Dr Twilite said. "Better than that draughty police station anyway. Now, who else is there?"

They went to the school to see how the children were. They found them all warm and snug and asleep in their classrooms, and decided it might be best not to disturb them, and so left them where they were.

Soon the streets were empty of people. The ones Dr and Mr Twilite had been unable to find addresses for they deposited in nearby shops. They carried several up to the bedding section in Stribberling's Department Store, lay them down on the beds, and covered them in blankets from the linen display. Stranger lay next to stranger, snoring away together like old friends, with large quantities of newspapers stuffed down their tights and up their vests.

"All nice and cosy!" Dr Twilite said. "No one's going to die of cold anyway, so no worries about that. And now they're all safe and warm, let's see if we can work out how to wake them up."

7

The Patchwork Bag

"Do we have to?" Mr Twilite asked. "Can't we just let them sleep till spring?"

"No, we must wake them," Dr Twilite said. "If we don't, they'll miss Christmas and New Year, and maybe even their birthdays."

"But how," Mr Twilite said, "do we do it?"

"Don't worry," Dr Twilite said. "I have an idea. We need to create some kind of great bang. Make a noise that no one can sleep through. Something to startle them all awake."

"But what can we make a bang like that with?" Mr Twilite demanded. "Short of finding some dynamite?"

"Simple," Dr Twilite said. "I was thinking about it as we cycled home. We just make a great enormous bag, fill it with air, tie it with string, and then we burst it! And the boom should wake everyone up!"

Mr Twilite thought it over. It seemed like a good idea, only:

"What do we make the bag with?" he asked.

"Whatever we've got," Dr Twilite said. "Let's see what's in the yard."

They went out to explore the scrap yard, and to inspect everything they had collected and which was still awaiting recycling.

"Right," Dr Twilite said, "now what have we here?"

There was no shortage of material with which to make the bag. There were heaps of vegetable scrapings, boxes of banana skins, stacks of orange peel, barrels of apple rind, bundles of waste paper, piles of rags and plastic carriers.

"Right," Dr Twilite said, "let's get everything out and start stitching. Now where's that squirrel?" (He was right behind her.) "Perkins," she said "kindly fetch the recycled sewing basket!" And he hopped off to get it.

They sewed by day and they sewed by night, and a great enormous patchwork bag slowly began to take shape. There were bits of everything in it—paper, cardboard, peelings, husks,

skins, leaves, tree-bark, old chewing-gum
wrappers, comics and magazines.

"Now sew up the sides," Dr Twilite said,
and on they stitched, ignoring the blisters on
their thumbs, until finally the bag was completed, and they were ready to fill it with air.

"But how are we going to inflate it?" Mr
Twilite asked. "It'll take for ever with a bicycle
pump."

But Dr Twilite had already thought of that.

"Don't worry!" she said. "The methane!"

"The what?"

"The cow pat gas," she said. "That we use
for the heating. We'll fill the bag up with that."

She led the way to the storage tank, topped up the supply of cow pats, connected up the pipes, and fed the gas into the enormous bag. Slowly it began to fill, taking on the appearance of a huge patchwork bouncy castle.

"It's a bouncy bag!" Mr Twilite cried in delight. "I've never seen a bouncy bag before. Let alone a recycled bouncy one."

"Almost full now," Dr Twilite said. "Have the recycled string ready."

Mr Twilite lassoed the neck of the bag with a coil of recycled string, he knotted it tightly to stop the gas from escaping, and soon it was all secure.

"Right," Dr Twilite said. "Phase one successfully completed. Now for phase two."

"And what's phase two?"

"Transportation," she said. "Get the bicycle. And while you're at it, watch that squirrel, he's sneaking off for a snooze."

"But wait," Mr Twilite objected. "Even with the bag filled up, how are we going to burst it? How are we going to make an enormous bang loud enough to wake everyone?"

"Easy!" Dr Twilite said. "A couple of rocks

and a great height should do the trick. You'll see. Come on. Let's get the bike."

The tandem was brought round to the yard, and the enormous patchwork bag was tied to it, and two sets of old pram wheels were placed under it so that it could be towed along.

"Where to?" Mr Twilite asked.

"Stribberling's Department Store," Dr Twilite said. "The roof!"

They got on to the tandem and cycled to town, towing the bag behind. It was a tight squeeze getting it over the bridge, but they managed, and then rode on along the empty streets to stop outside Stribberling's Department Store, the

tallest building in Callender Hill. It wasn't so tall by big city standards, but by Callender Hill standards it was very tall indeed, and all of six storeys high.

"Right," Dr Twilite said. "Leave the bag out here. Tether it down, to stop it blowing away, and then let's get those two big rocks we brought out of the saddle-bags. Here, give me a hand."

Mr Twilite secured the bag, tying it between two lamp posts to prevent it from floating off.

"OK," Dr Twilite said. "Into Stribberling's now, and on to the roof."

Dr and Mr Twilite picked up a rock each,

put them into the rucksacks they had brought, and went into the store. Perkins bounded along behind them, carrying a small piece of gravel he had brought to show willing.

Up they went on the escalators, all the way to the top. On every floor of the shop, people were fast asleep. Assistants stood behind the counters, their heads resting on the tills. Snoring customers waited to be served.

"This is as far as the escalator goes," Mr Twilite said. "But we're not at the top yet."

"The stairs," Dr Twilite said. "This way."

They passed a sign which said "No Entry. Staff Only" and went on up some stairs until they came to a door marked "Access To Roof. Authorized Personnel Only."

"Are we authorized personnel then?" Mr Twilite asked.

"We are now," Dr Twilite said. "Come on."

They pushed the door open and went out on to the roof. There, far beneath them, was the great enormous patchwork bag—only from where they were, it looked much smaller now.

"I feel dizzy!" Mr Twilite said.

"Careful, don't fall. It's only a low parapet."

But the warning came too late for Perkins, who had been scampering about on the ledge with no apparent fear of heights at all. He lost his footing and over he went, falling without a sound, as he plummeted towards the road.

"Oh no!" Mr Twilite screamed. "Poor Perkins! He'll be killed!"

But he was nothing of the sort. He landed on the enormous bag. And being too small to burst it, he simply bounced up into the air again, all the way back to the top of the roof.

"Grab him!" Dr Twilite said. "Get him on the rebound. But don't fall off yourself!"

Dr Twilite held on to Mr Twilite's belt and Mr Twilite made a grab for Perkins as he bounced back up to the top floor.

"Ahh!" he said. "Missed him by a tail!" And down he went again. And Dr Twilite noticed that he seemed to be smiling.

"You know," she said, "I think he's enjoying this."

Down Perkins went for a second time, hit the bag again, and started his second journey up.

"Be sure to get him!" Dr Twilite said. "If he goes down for a third time, there's a good chance he won't come back up. Hold on to my recycled bloomers and I'll try to grab him myself."

Mr Twilite gripped Dr Twilite's bloomers tightly by the patch and she leant out over the parapet as Perkins came up. By now there was a fixed grin on his hairy features.

"Look at him," Mr Twilite said. "He's addicted to bouncing."

Perkins seemed all set to go down yet again, but Dr Twilite got a hand around his tail.

"Gotcha!" she cried, and she pulled him back to the safety of the roof.

"Now sit there, Perkins, and don't fall off again. You're getting far too frisky. You're not supposed to do things like that without a parachute. Now, where are the rocks?"

Dr Twilite picked up one of the rocks they had brought, and staggered with it to the parapet.

"Hold on to me," she said. And Mr Twilite held her by the coat tails this time, as he was afraid her bloomers might tear. "OK, I'll just take aim, and—here we go!"

Dr Twilite let the rock drop. Then she jumped back and ducked under the parapet.

"Quick! Fingers in your ears," she said. "Or the bang will deafen you!" And she stuck

Perkins's tail into one of his ears to protect it. He couldn't hear anything out of the other ear, as he had managed to get an acorn stuck in it. Dr Twilite kept meaning to take him to the vet, but at the moment the vet was asleep.

"OK, ready for the bang!"

But there was no bang. Just a muzzled thump, followed by a big empty silence.

Dr Twilite sneaked a look over the parapet. There, down below her, was the enormous bag, and next to it the rock lay on the pavement, having missed the bag by inches.

"Drat," she said. "Missed. Let's try again."

So Mr Twilite grabbed her by the coat tails, and over went the second rock. Again they dived for cover.

This time there was the most enormous bang Callender Hill had ever heard. It echoed and clattered from building to building, and street to street. It boomed in ladies' handbags, it echoed in gentlemen's pockets, it crashed down the drains and clanged around the sewers and terrified all the rats.

Dr Twilite took her fingers out of her ears. Even though they had muffled the sound, her head was spinning. She looked at Mr Twilite.

"Well, if that doesn't wake them," she said, "nothing will. I'm sure a big bang will do it. It's my big bang theory."

She went to the parapet and gazed down into the street. But the great, enormous recycled patchwork bag was gone, shattered into a million tiny fragments, and blown away, all over the town.

8

Awake

Sam Walker woke up and yawned. Where was he? Oh, no! He hadn't fallen asleep in class! He'd get it in the neck all right now from Mr Stewart. A good long lecture on the virtues of going to bed early. If only . . .

But when Sam looked around him, he saw that everybody else was yawning and stretching, as if they had just woken up too.

Ah, well, now that wasn't so bad. If Mr Stewart's lessons were getting to be so boring that he sent the whole class to sleep—

Mr Stewart!

Even he was yawning and stretching as if he had just woken up. And that wasn't all. Oh no. Far from it. It was worse than that.

Mr Stewart had grown a beard!

Grown a beard! However had he managed it? Sam had dozed off and Mr Stewart had been clean-shaven. He had woken up a few seconds later and Mr Stewart had grown a beard! But how had he done that? In only a few moments?

But it wasn't just that. Not only had Mr Stewart grown a beard—there was a spider's web hanging from it too!

Had Mr Stewart noticed?

Well, he seemed a bit embarrassed to start with. Embarrassed that he could have dozed off in front of the whole class. Best, maybe, just to carry on, he thought, as if nothing had happened. Just get on with what he had been saying.

Only, what had he been saying? Oh yes, something about hibernation.

"OK, class," he began, and for some reason his mouth felt very dry, "now I believe we were discussing—"

He went to scratch his chin. It was a habit of Mr Stewart's to scratch his chin when he was talking. Nothing unusual about that. Only this time, when he went to scratch his chin, there was hair on it. And his fingernails, which he usually chewed to bits, were long.

Hair on his chin? HAIR ON IT! Long finger-nails?

But how could he have hair on his chin? He'd only just shaved it that morning. It took days, weeks even, to grow a beard!

"Just get on with some reading," he told the class. "I'm going to have a quick word with the headmaster."

As soon as he was gone, Sam Walker turned to Simone Drew and said:

"I don't know about you, but I'm starving. I feel as if I haven't eaten for weeks! I'm going to sneak a sandwich before Mr Stewart gets back."

Sam nipped out to the cloakroom, grabbed his lunch-box, opened it up and reached inside.

But his hand stopped when the smell hit him. His cheese roll had grown whiskers and had developed green spots.

"Eeech!" he said. "It's gone mouldy! But how could it? My mum made it fresh this morning."

Dr and Mr Twilite took the down escalator and headed for the ground floor. All around them the staff and customers of Stribberling's Department Store were waking and stretching and picking up where they had left off.

Dr Twilite had Perkins hidden in her coat pocket. Two people with a squirrel might arouse suspicion, and she didn't want to arouse any of that.

They caught another escalator and went on down through the bedding department, where the people they had laid on the beds were beginning to wake.

"I'm most awfully sorry, I must have dozed off."

"How very embarrassing! In bed with a complete stranger, and we haven't even been introduced."

On one bed a fight was narrowly avoided when the man lying on it accused the lady next to him of putting newspapers up his trousers.

"Is this your idea of a joke, is it? Stuffing old newspapers up a bloke's trousers when he nods off for a couple of winks. I was only trying the bed out to see if it was comfy. I suppose you think this is funny!"

"Oh dear," Dr Twilite said. "I do hope there isn't going to be trouble."

So they quickly and discreetly left the store and headed for their bicycle.

Meanwhile, round in Miss Endicott's house, Sergeant Porter began to stir upon the sofa, just as Tiddles woke in his basket, and as Miss Endicott—in her armchair—opened a watery eye.

"My memory," Miss Endicott thought, as she woke, "is definitely on the blink. I could have sworn that I was in the police station, having a word with that big dozy sergeant about the shortage of cow pats—"

Her thoughts were interrupted by the sound of yawning coming from the sofa as Sergeant

Porter stirred—heavily, like a spoon in treacle.

"Good heavens," he thought. "I must have dozed off at my duties, right at my very desk. I was talking to that batty old woman, wasn't I? The one with the stinky dog. And what was the latest bee in her bonnet? Oh yes, cow pats. Well—"

Then Sergeant Porter realized that he wasn't behind his desk any more. He was lying on a sofa in an unfamiliar room, which smelt of mothballs and lavender. And when he looked about he saw—yes—a dog in a basket— looking just like that Miss Endicott's dog. What was it called now? Piddles or Niddles or—and who was that in the armchair? Looking rather like—

Just as Sergeant Porter saw Miss Endicott, she saw him. And while Sergeant Porter—who was trained to deal with emergencies—merely blinked in surprise, Miss Endicott let out a loud scream.

"Ahhhh!" she cried. "A burglar! Quick, Tiddles! Seize! Sink your fangs into him! Bark for the police!"

Tiddles didn't actually have much by way of

fangs. The only teeth he had were false ones, and he certainly wasn't going to risk them on anything as tough-looking as Sergeant Porter. So instead of seizing him as he was told, he went and hid under the sideboard.

"You cowardly beast!" Miss Endicott shouted. "Desert me, would you, in my hour of need. Very well, I'll deal with this thug myself." And she took up the poker from the fireplace.

"Now hang on, madam," Sergeant Porter said. "I'm sure there's a perfectly simple explanation for all this."

"Rob an old lady, would you!" Miss Endicott cried. "Steal the very comfort from her sofa, eh? Come in here in your great big boots! Treading mud everywhere! After my valuables, are you? Well, don't you dare move, or you'll feel the cold steel of this poker in your ribs. Stay there while I ring for the police."

"But, madam," Sergeant Porter said, "if you look closely, you'll see that I am the police. It's me. Sergeant Porter. Your friend."

Miss Endicott kept hold of the poker while she took a good look at the man on her sofa. Finally she put it down.

"Well, Sergeant Porter. It *is* you. Good heavens. And you've followed me home. Well, well."

"And to be honest," he said, "I don't understand how I got here. One moment I was at my desk in the police station. The next thing, I'm here on the sofa."

He and Miss Endicott both looked very perplexed for a moment, but then she brightened up.

"I think I know what it is, Sergeant," she said, "and why you followed me home."

"You do?"

"Oh, yes. I think, Sergeant Porter, that you must have fallen in love."

"I have?" he said. "Are you sure?"

"Positive. Because that's how people act when they are in love. They don't know what they're doing or where they are half the time."

Sergeant Porter scratched his head.

"But who," he said, "could I have fallen in love with?" He looked about, and his eyes fell on Tiddles. "Not that dog, surely."

"Not the dog!" Miss Endicott said. "*Me.*"

"*You?*" said Sergeant Porter.

"Yes. I know you are rather young for me," Miss Endicott said. "And though I can't say that I love you too, I'll try to make the effort. You can put up in the spare room for now, and take the bins out on Fridays, and we'll get married in a couple of weeks."

"But," said Sergeant Porter, "I—"

But Miss Endicott was already opening her diary. "Now, when would be a good day for the wedding?" she asked. "Would a Tuesday suit you? I can't make it on a Monday, I'm afraid, as that's when I collect my pension."

"But to be honest," Sergeant Porter objected, "I don't feel as if I am in love with you at all. And I can't get married on Tuesday or any other day, as I'm married already."

Miss Endicott picked up the poker again. Tiddles retreated further under the sideboard.

"Why, you beast!" she cried. "Trifle with a woman's affections, would you! Come round here in your big boots and break a woman's heart. Telling her you love her madly, and then saying you're already married. Leave my house this instant!"

"I wouldn't mind pushing off, actually,"

Sergeant Porter said, "if it's all the same to you. They'll be wondering where I am down at the station."

"Go then," Miss Endicott said. "But don't think you've heard the last of this. I shall be on to the papers about you. You—rotter!"

"If you'll excuse me then, madam," Sergeant Porter said, and straightening his notebook, he hurried to the door.

"Yes, go!" Miss Endicott said. "And never darken my carpets again."

Sergeant Porter went off down the path.

"Very sorry," he muttered. "Can't think how I got here. Perfectly rational explanation, I'm sure. Get to the bottom of it soon. Rely on me."

"And another thing!" Miss Endicott bellowed after him. "What about the cow pats?"

But Sergeant Porter was away round the corner. As he hurried along, he saw that the world about him was coming to life, looking as puzzled and confused as he felt.

"Where am I?" people said. "What happened? How did I get here? I don't half feel hungry. I could eat a horse. And a jockey for afters."

And before doing anything else, they hurried off to the chip shop in the High Street, banged on the door, and shouted:

"Come on in there, wake those chips up! Give those sausages a nudge, and get those peas moving. Tell your fish to get their fingers out. We're absolutely starving!"

9

The Great Stay Awake Mixture

When Sergeant Porter got back to the police station, his boss Inspector Rogers sent for him to come to his office. Sergeant Porter found the Inspector there, shaving with an electric razor.

"Ah, there you are, Porter," Inspector Rogers said. "It looks like we have a mystery on our hands. Two weeks have gone missing, as you may have noticed. Two weeks have completely vanished out of the life of every man, woman, child, dog, cat and goldfish in this town. I want you to get out there and look for them."

"Two weeks, sir?" Sergeant Porter said. "And what would this missing two weeks look like, exactly?"

"Well, you know what two weeks in autumn usually look like, Sergeant—a bit cold, a bit foggy, a bit damp."

"And where do you think I should start looking, sir?"

"Start with lost property and go on from there. But you'd better find them. I've had the Superintendent on the phone. He says we can't have two weeks go missing and do nothing about it. So see if you can't track them down. And when you've got them, bring them back so that we may return them to their rightful owners, who have been robbed of their time."

"If you say so, sir—"

"I do. Though, strictly speaking, it's not just two weeks. There's ten thousand people in Callender Hill, and they've all lost two weeks each. So that's twenty thousand weeks altogether, which, if you divide by fifty-two, makes about"—he poked at his calculator—"four hundred and fifty-three years we're looking for altogether."

"Four hundred and fifty-three years, sir!" Sergeant Porter gasped. "Well, where could you hide a great chunk of time like that?"

"Search me, Sergeant," the Inspector said.

"Very well, sir. Perhaps you'd like to begin by emptying your pockets."

"No, no, I don't mean search me search *me*. I mean, search me, I don't know. You'd better go and start looking."

"Right, sir," he said. "I will."

"I hate waste of any sort," Dr Twilite said, "and that's why I feel so bad about it. Because time wasted is one of the greatest wastes of all. You never get it back and you can't recycle it either. Of course I blame myself, for ever making that hibernation mixture in the first place. But if certain people hadn't poured certain other people's mixtures down the well, we wouldn't have got into this mess."

Mr Twilite looked sheepish. So sheepish he almost went "Baa!"

"Sorry," he said, "but I wasn't to know."

"I suppose not," Dr Twilite said. "But all the same, it's two weeks gone for ever. Just think, in that two weeks someone might have painted a beautiful picture or invented a cure for hiccups. I can see this hibernation idea of mine maybe wasn't such a good one after all."

"I don't see what we can do about it now," Mr Twilite said. "As you say, once time is gone, it's gone. You can't ever bring it back."

"True," Dr Twilite said. "But as everyone has been asleep for two weeks, well, if we could somehow keep them *awake* for two weeks now, that might even up the score."

"How can we keep them awake for two weeks?" Mr Twilite asked. "Have a noisy party, do you mean?"

"No," Dr Twilite said. "I was thinking more of a mixture of some sort, a Great Stay Awake Mixture. Now, what could I make it of?"

"Now just a moment, my dear," Mr Twilite protested, "I wouldn't rush into anything."

But Dr Twilite was already on her way to her workshop.

Sergeant Porter spent two weeks looking for the missing two weeks, but he didn't find them.

"Good time thrown after bad," he said. "That's four weeks I've lost now. Time spent looking for time lost is just more time wasted."

He looked everywhere, and he visited all the known criminals in the area to see if they had pinched the two weeks and hidden them under the floorboards in bags marked SWAG. But no.

"We don't go in for bags marked SWAG any more," Fingers Smithers told him. "It's all computers now. And anyway, I've done my

It's all computers now

time. So why should I want to pinch any more?"

And Sergeant Porter went away disappointed.

Sam and Lorna were up all that first night. After two weeks asleep, they didn't feel tired in the least. Their school's headmaster announced that there would be a few days' holiday, to make up for the weekends they had missed. But then he said there would also be extra homework, to catch up on the lessons which had not been done.

Miss Conway and Mr Stewart both set projects entitled:

"What I Did While I Was Asleep For Two Weeks."

Sam wrote a one-word essay.

"Snored," he wrote.

"You are supposed," Mr Stewart said coldly, "to use your imagination."

And he didn't shave his new beard off, because for some reason he imagined it suited him.

Nobody ever did discover why the people in Callender Hill had fallen asleep. And as for Dr and Mr Twilite, they said nothing, as they were afraid of getting into trouble.

"We meant well, though, my dear," Mr Twilite said. "Do you think we ought to tell them it was us?"

"In a word," said Dr Twilite, "no. Now if you'll excuse me, I'll get back to my Great Stay Awake Mixture. I just want to stir in a couple of recycled alarm clocks, and a few early morning phone calls, along with a tape recording of two cats fighting in a dustbin. Then it should be ready."

Shortly afterwards, when dusk began to fall, Dr Twilite could be seen stealing down to the end of the garden, carrying a big bucket of a mixture which bubbled strangely. She set the bucket down by the old well, lifted the cover off, and poured the entire contents in. Then she replaced the cover, and made sure it was shut tight.

"There," she said. "That should perk them up. If that Great Stay Awake Mixture doesn't give them a bit of time back, nothing will."

And down in the well, the Great Stay Awake Mixture seeped away into the underground stream. And the stream carried it to the river, and the river flowed to the reservoir. And at length the mixture got into the water supply.

And everyone drank it.

"I can't get to sleep," Lorna Walker said later that night.

"Just try," her mum told her.

"But I have tried! I've been trying for ages. And the harder I try, the more it keeps me awake. I just don't feel sleepy at all."

"Neither do I, Mum," called a second voice. It was Sam, wide awake too.

"It's almost ten o'clock," Mum said. "If you can't get to sleep, count some sheep."

"I've already counted them."

"So count them again. And make sure that you haven't missed any."

Mum went back to the living room and joined Dad on the sofa in front of the TV.

"I hope they're not going to be awake for the rest of the night," he said.

But they weren't. At least not just for the rest of the night.

They were awake for the next two weeks.

Dr Twilite went out with her wheelbarrow to start the morning's work. It was a beautiful mellow autumn day, and there was an abundance of ripeness everywhere, turning to decay.

"There's everything here you could possibly need," she said. "Cow pats, spiders' webs and all the rest. Yes, it's the autumn life for me. The winter's too cold, the summer's too hot, and the spring's just far too springy. Yes, autumn is the best time of all."

Red berries were on the holly bushes by then, and there was a covering of mist on the ground.

"I'll have to start gathering that mist," Dr Twilite thought. "I'll bag it up, dye it pink, add a bit of sugar, put it on sticks, and sell it as candy floss. And I'm so glad I thought of the Great Stay Awake Mixture," she said. "It makes things up to people. They'll appreciate that."

But that was only what she thought. She couldn't hear the babies crying—the ones who had been crying for ten days non-stop, and who still had another four days to go.

"Do you think it was a good idea, Perkins?" she said.

But as for Perkins the squirrel, well, yes—he had fallen asleep.

No one quite knows how he managed it, as he had been poked regularly, and he had been given some of the Great Stay Awake Mixture too. But even that was not enough.

He was sitting on the handle of the wheel-barrow when hibernation overtook him. First one eye closed, then the other, and then he was gone, snoring away, all wrapped up in his tail.

"I'll put him up in the airing cupboard," Dr Twilite thought. "Leave him there where it's warm."

So she wrapped him up in a dishcloth, put him in a box and set him in the airing cupboard. He slept there all through the winter, and didn't wake till spring. And when he did awake, a few months later, he couldn't, for the life of him, remember where he had hidden his nuts.

But that was no real surprise to anyone.